Topsy + Tim
School Adventures

Jean and Gareth Adamson

Blackie Children's Books

It's the summer term and Topsy and Tim are going back to school.
Are we still in Miss Terry's class, Mum?
Yes, until the summer holidays.
I want to sit next to Tony Welch.

In the school playground they see their friends.
Hi Topsy!
There's Kerry, Mum.
There's Tony!

Hello, Kerry. Did you have a nice holiday?
Yes, thank you.

Mum kisses the twins.
Have a lovely day. See you this afternoon.

It's time to go in. Miss Terry rings the bell.
Line up, please, everyone.
Bye, Mum.
Bye!

The twins hang up their coats.
Wait for me, Topsy.
Here's my peg.
TOPSY
TIM
KERRY
STEVE

In the classroom they find their places.
Your name is on top of your pile of books.
You're here, Topsy!
Tim, you're here, next to me.

Then Miss Terry asks the children about their holidays.
Tim and I went horse-riding, Miss Terry!

I've painted a picture of the farm, Miss Terry.

At playtime they chat to their friends.

D'you want to come to tea at our house, Kerry?

My painting's gone!

Miss Terry, where's my farm picture?

Everyone searches for the painting.

Mum comes to collect the children.
Hello!
I've lost my painting, Mum.

Is this it? I found it outside in the bushes.
Yes, it's mine! Look, Miss Terry.

It must have blown out of the window. Off you go. See you tomorrow.
Bye, Miss Terry!

The next morning it's time for school again.
Don't forget your gym bag, Tim.
Hurry up! Your plimsolls are on the bed.

On the way to school Topsy and Tim stop to call for Kerry.
Good morning, Twins!
Have you remembered your gym shoes?
Yes, thanks, we have.
I can't wait for gym, it's brilliant!

I want to win a gym badge this term.
You've got one, haven't you, Tim?
Yes. This is my gym badge. I got it last term. I'm good at gym.

At school...
Hang your shoe bags on your pegs, children.

When I've taken the register you can all change for gym.

Soon it is time to change.
Miss Terry, can you help me with my shoelaces?

In the gym Miss Terry starts with a warm-up.
First of all I want you to pretend you are a bee buzzing around a garden...
I'm going to sting you!
Bzzz. Bzzz.

After the warm-up...
Now get in your teams and we'll use the apparatus.
Hurray!

Each team helps to get out a different piece of apparatus.
That's right, Tim. I'll just check it's fixed.
This mat is heavy!

Then it is time to start.
Look, Miss Terry. I can balance!

After a while Miss Terry lets the class have a game of 'Pirates'.
Remember, the floor is the sea full of sharks. The apparatus is the land. If you touch the floor you're out!

Oooh, help!

You're out, Topsy.

Now I won't win a gym badge like Tim.

The 'Pirates' game stops.
We'll finish with some handstands.

Very good, Kerry.

Well tried, Topsy!

At the end of gym...
....and today's gym badge goes to Kerry. Well done, Kerry!
Well, I'm going to try to win next time!

A week later the class are going on a nature walk with Miss Terry and some of the parents.
Now, remember... Don't pick the wildflowers and stay on the footpath.

The children set off along a country footpath.
Does anyone know what kind of tree this is?
Oooh, I do, Miss Terry. It's an oak tree.

I'm going to collect some twigs and leaves from the ground.

Let's do a bark rubbing, Kerry.

Look at this spider's web, Miss Terry.

Yes, Stevie. And that spider has caught a fly.

Tony and I are drawing a picture of these pink flowers, Miss.

Tim watches a butterfly drinking from a flower.

The butterfly flies away. Tim follows it.
Come back butterfly!

Suddenly...
Aaaagh! What's happening!

Tim has walked into a bog.
Mum! Miss Terry! I'm stuck!

Mum and Miss Terry run to the spot...
Keep still, Tim!

Mum stands on firm ground and pulls!

My wellies are stuck in the mud!

I can fish them out with the end of my stick.

Ooooh, look. They're very muddy.

Pooh! Tim. Smelly wellies.
Don't be silly, Topsy. Now follow me and remember- keep to the path!

They come to a pond.
That's a moorhen.
Look at that big bird, Topsy!
Try to keep very still.

Miss Terry fishes for frogspawn.
There's a frog, Miss Terry.

These are frogs' eggs. We'll take a few back to the class.

Miss Terry fishes out other tiny creatures.
Now, have a look at these before I put them back in the pond.

Back in school Miss Terry puts the frogspawn in the aquarium.
Each black dot grows a tail and turns into a wriggly tadpole. The tadpole turns into a frog.
They talk about the leaves and twigs...
Miss, look!
Can you remember the name of that tree, Tim?
Yes, it's an oak tree.
Miss Terry puts the sketches and rubbings on the wall.
Well done, everyone!
That's ours, Kerry.

A few days later Miss Terry talks to the class.
Hands up if you would like to be in a play?

The play is about a farmer and his animals.
Tim, you can be the pig.
Oink! Oink!

Topsy, you can be the farmer's goose. You must flap your wings.
Like this, Miss Terry!

Miss Terry chooses the farmer next.
Roger, you are big and strong. You can be the farmer.
Yeah!

Once the children have their parts they gather round the piano.
We're going to practise the song.
What are we going to do now, Miss Terry?

Everyone sings the song making their own animal noise or movement.
With a Moo, Miaow, Woof, Quack ....
Baaa! Baaa!
Cluck! Cluck!
Moo! Moo!
Quack! Quack!
Woof! Woof!
Miaow! Miaow!

The next day the children make animal masks to wear in the play.
I can't see, Miss Terry.
Keep still, Topsy. I'm just making this the right size.

There now! Now it has a hole to see through, and a beak.

I'll paint its eyes blue, and its beak yellow.

Next Miss Terry helps Tim to make a pig mask.

Now we make ears from this stiff paper and a nose from a paper cup.

I'll paint it piggy pink.

When the mask is dry, Tim paints a big smile on the nose.

Once all the masks are ready the children put them on and practise their play.
Oink! Oink!

That afternoon Topsy and Tim take home their invitation.
It's an invitation to our play.
This is for you and Dad!
A play! What fun!

That night Dad reads the children a story.

Are you coming to our play, Dad?
I'm a pig and Topsy's a goose.
Yes, I'll come if I can.

The day of the play arrives. The children get ready.
Roger, you need to have a red nose and a big moustache.

When the play is over the children bow. Topsy's hat falls off.

It's nearly the end of term. Topsy and Tim are practising for the school sports.
Hurry up, Topsy! We won't win anything if you're so slow.
I can go faster than you can!

No, you can't. I'm the fastest runner in the whole class.
Oh no you're not! I can run as fast as you, so there!

Soon there is trouble.
Mum! Tim pulled my hair.

Mum stops the fight.
Now stop all this squabbling! School Sports Days are meant to be fun.

Soon it's time for Sports Day. Topsy and Tim are still squabbling over who is the faster of the two...
Look, there are Topsy and Tim!
We'll soon see who is the fastest runner. The running race is first.

Everyone lines up to start the first race.
Ready, steady...GO!

Both Topsy and Tim fall in the race.
Hurrah! I've won.
Oh! I tripped.
Ooh! Ouch!

Never mind, you two. There are plenty more races.

Next it is the skipping race.

The twins get their ropes in a tangle.

Then there is the sack race.
Don't bump me, Topsy!
Oh. help! I can't see!

The next race is for mums. It is the egg and spoon race.
Ready, steady..GO!

They all run very fast.
Mum has won!
Hurrah!
I've done it!

After the mums' race it is the 'Three-legged race'.
We must have you two together. You are the perfect pair!

The other children in the race are all bigger than Topsy and Tim, but they do not make neat pairs.
...And now it is time for the children's three-legged race.

The race is on! Topsy and Tim run together easily.
We've done it. Hurray!

At the end the headmistress presents the prizes.
Well run, Topsy and Tim.

BLACKIE CHILDREN'S BOOKS

Published by the Penguin Group
Penguin Books Ltd, 27 Wrights Lane, London W8 5TZ, England
Penguin Books USA Inc., 375 Hudson Street, New York, New York 10014, USA
Penguin Books Australia Ltd, Ringwood, Victoria, Australia
Penguin Books Canada Ltd, 10 Alcorn Avenue, Toronto, Ontario, Canada M4V 3B2
Penguin Books (NZ) Ltd, 182-190 Wairau Road, Auckland 10, New Zealand

Penguin Books Ltd, Registered Offices: Harmondsworth, Middlesex, England

First published 1994 by Blackie Children's Books
1 3 5 7 9 10 8 6 4 2

Novelisation by Carol Watson

Made and printed in Hong Kong by Imago

A CIP catalogue record for this book is available from the British Library

ISBN 0 216 94157 1